*For the sweetest little granddaughter
that anyone could ever ask for.*

Hello! My name is Hillary Eleanor
and I have a very special Grandma.

Listen carefully and I'll tell you why. . .

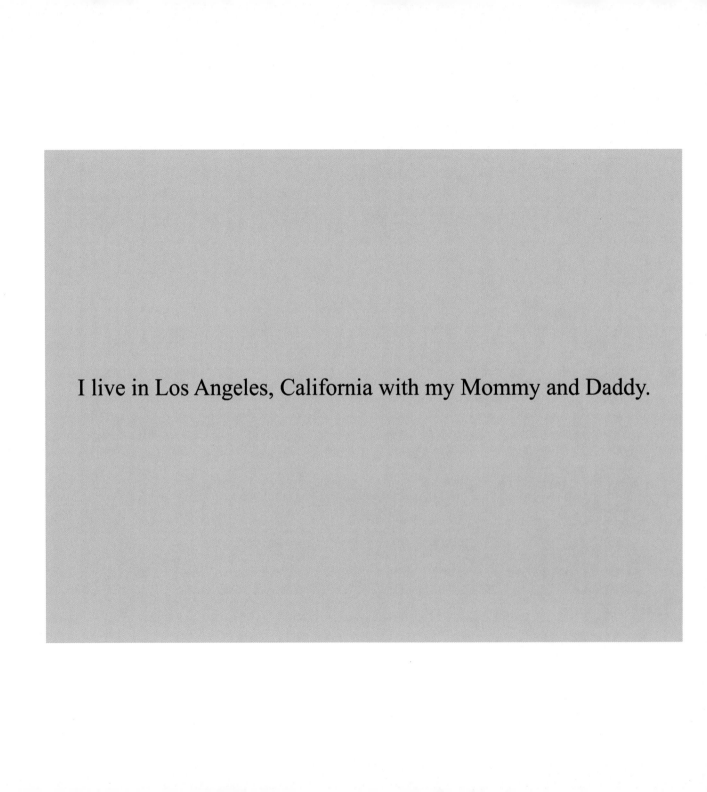

I live in Los Angeles, California with my Mommy and Daddy.

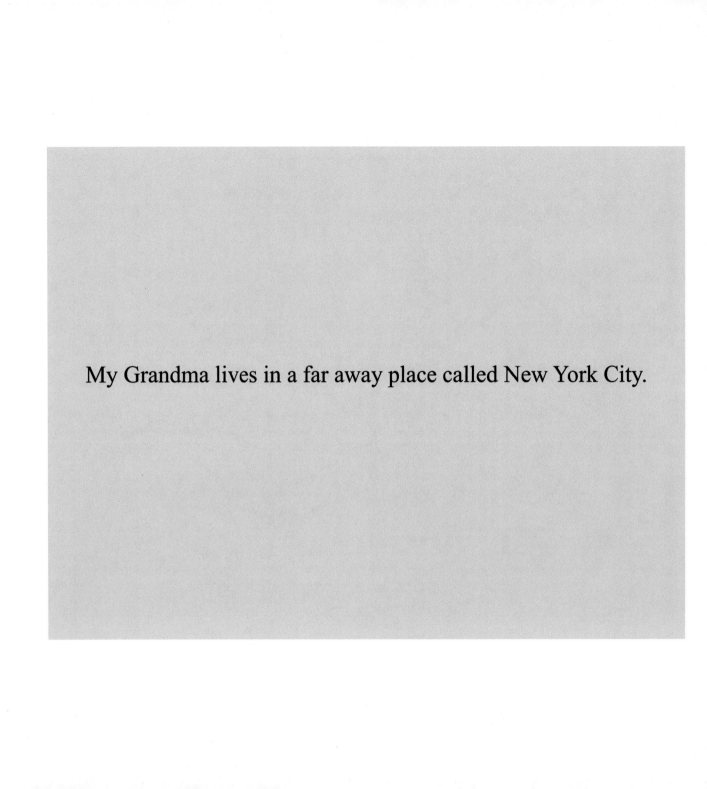

My Grandma lives in a far away place called New York City.

Grandma came to visit me right after I was born. I was only two weeks old then! I was so little!

When it was time for Grandma to go back home, she was very sad to say goodbye. "Hillary Eleanor, I'm going to miss you very, very much," she said. "But even though I live so far away, we can still see each other every day. We can video chat on Mommy's cell phone!"

That's exactly what we did.
And suddenly my Grandma became….

"TV Grandma!"

Now that I'm a little older, Mommy, Daddy and I video chat with TV Grandma all the time.

I show her all the new things that I've learned to do.

Look TV Grandma, I can feed myself!

Look TV Grandma, I'm a Ballerina!

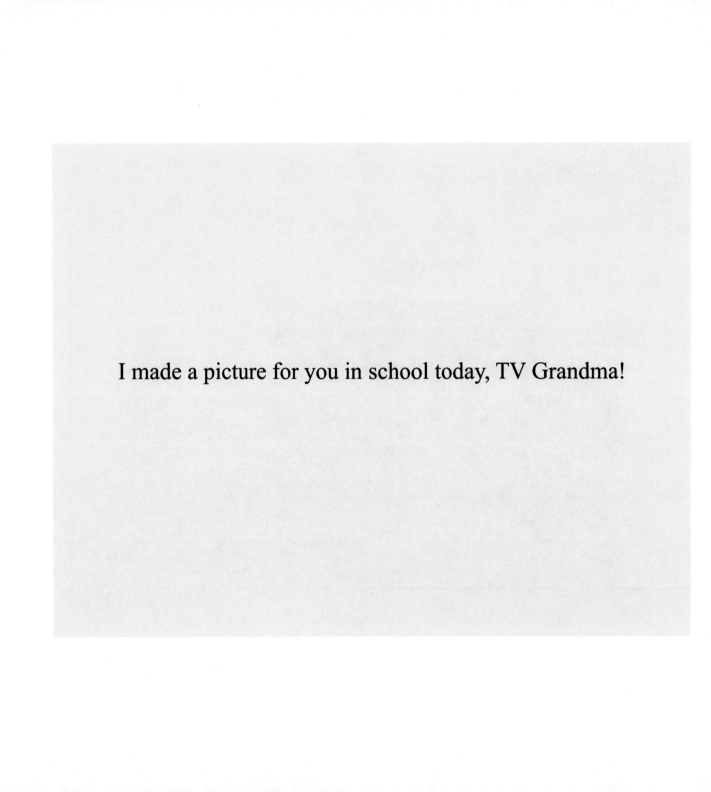

I made a picture for you in school today, TV Grandma!

TV Grandma loves to see all the new things that I've learned to do and tells me that she's very proud of me.

When it's time for us to say goodbye. . .

TV Grandma throws me lots of kisses and lots of computer hugs.

Soon, TV Grandma will be getting on a big airplane and coming to visit me.

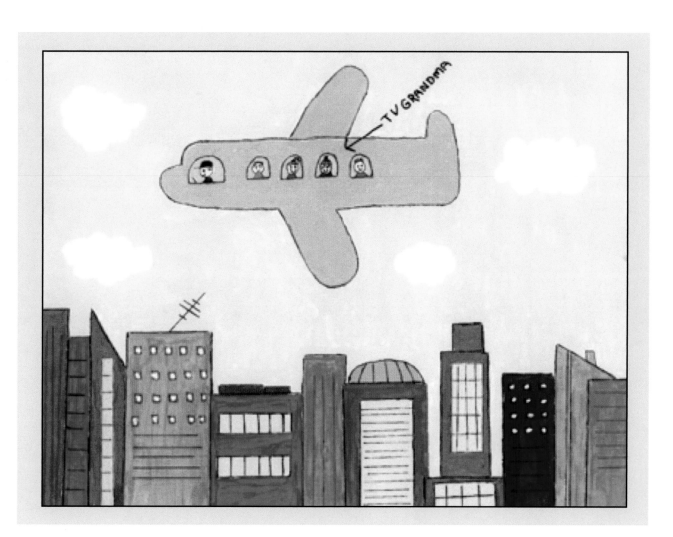

"Hillary Eleanor, don't be scared when you see me in person," TV Grandma said. "I'm much bigger than I seem to be on Mommy's cell phone. I'm just about the same size as your Mommy!"

I said, "I love you TV Grandma! I could never be scared of you!"

When the big day came, Mommy, Daddy and I went to pick up TV Grandma from the airport.

When I saw her I said, "TV Grandma, you were right! You are much bigger in person! That means there is so much more of you for me to love!!!"

TV Grandma laughed and laughed. Then she scooped me up in her arms and gave me lots of real kisses and lots of real hugs.

And that's why I have a very special Grandma!

The End!

Made in the USA
Middletown, DE
13 June 2023

32513829R00020